ISBN 0-590-99808-0

Text copyright © 1994 by Henrietta Stickland.
Illustrations copyright © 1994 by Paul Stickland.
All rights reserved. Published by Scholastic Inc., 555 Broadway, New York, NY 10012, by arrangement with Dutton Children's Books, a division of Penguin Books USA Inc.

12 11 10 9 8 7 6 5 4 3 2 1   6 7 8 9/9 0 1/0
Printed in the U.S.A.   08

DINOSAUR ROAR!

PAUL & HENRIETTA STICKLAND

Scholastic Inc.

New York Toronto London Auckland Sydney

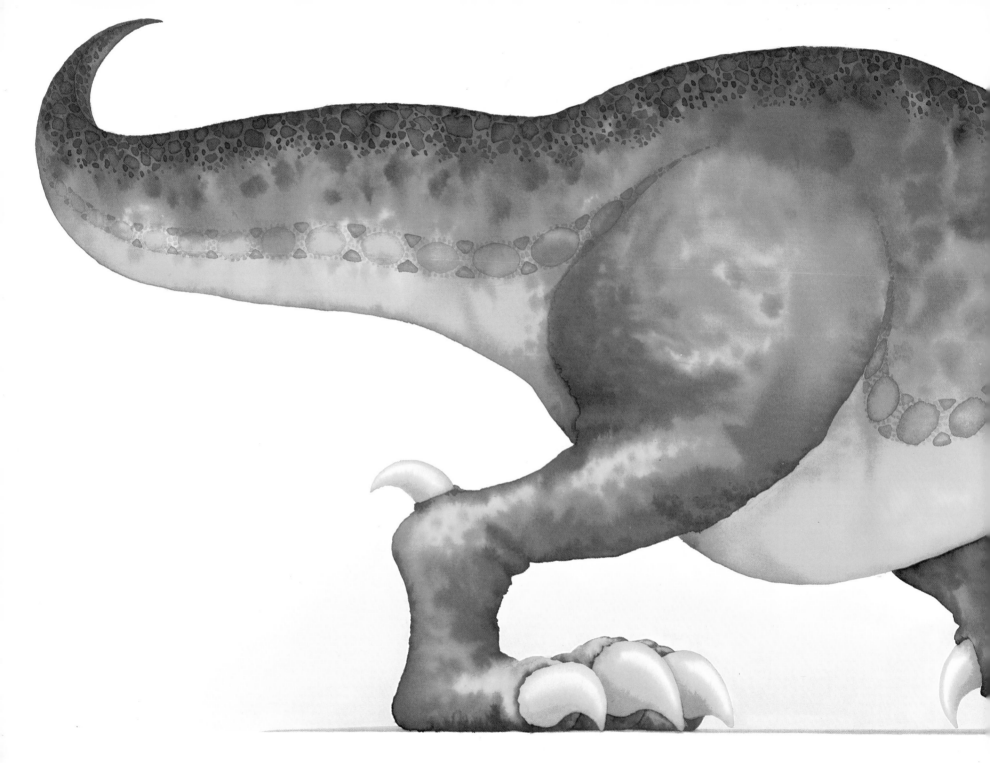

Dinosaur roar,

dinosaur squeak,

dinosaur fierce,

dinosaur meek,

dinosaur fast,

dinosaur slow,

dinosaur above

and dinosaur below.

Dinosaur weak,

dinosaur strong,

dinosaur short

or very, very long.

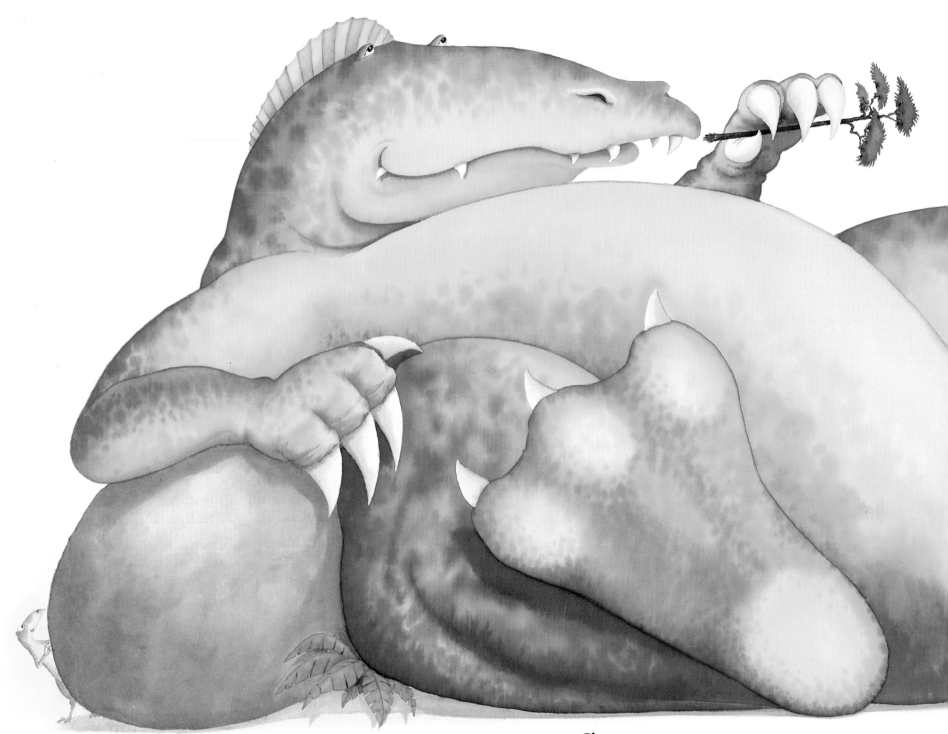

Dinosaur fat,

dinosaur tiny,

dinosaur clean

and dinosaur slimy.

Dinosaur sweet,

dinosaur grumpy,

dinosaur spiky

and dinosaur lumpy.

All sorts of dinosaurs

eating their lunch,

gobble, gobble, nibble, nibble,

munch, munch, scrunch!